TRACE
THEN COLOR

CARTOON
MERMAIDS,
UNICORNS,
AND OTHER CUTE STUFF

A TRACING AND COLORING BOOK FOR KIDS

KEVIN COULSTON
FirstArtBooks.com

Trace Then Color: Mermaids, Unicorns, and Other Cute Stuff

A Tracing and Coloring Book for Kids

© 2022 Kevin Coulston

ISBN: 9798354908776

THIS BOOK BELONGS TO:

_____

TRACE THEN COLOR
THE CUTE CHARACTER

TRACE THEN COLOR
THE CUTE CHARACTER

TRACE THEN COLOR
THE CUTE CHARACTER

TRACE THEN COLOR
THE CUTE CHARACTER

TRACE THEN COLOR
THE CUTE CHARACTER

TRACE THEN COLOR THE CUTE CHARACTER

TRACE THEN COLOR
THE CUTE CHARACTER

TRACE THEN COLOR
THE CUTE CHARACTER

TRACE THEN COLOR
THE CUTE CHARACTER

TRACE THEN COLOR
THE CUTE CHARACTER

TRACE THEN COLOR
THE CUTE CHARACTER

TRACE THEN COLOR
THE CUTE CHARACTER

TRACE THEN COLOR
THE CUTE CHARACTER

TRACE THEN COLOR
THE CUTE CHARACTER

TRACE THEN COLOR
THE CUTE CHARACTER

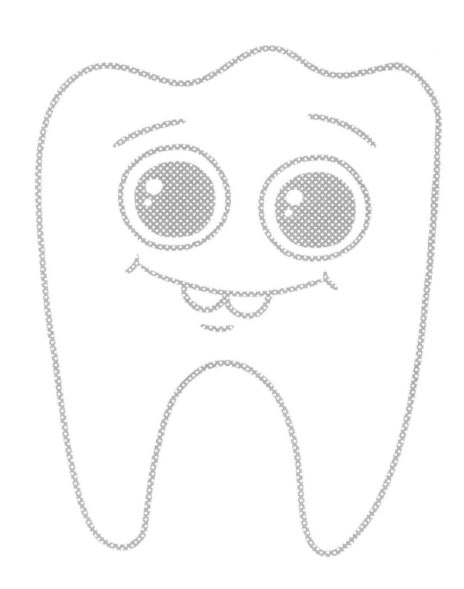

TRACE THEN COLOR
THE CUTE CHARACTER

TRACE THEN COLOR
THE CUTE CHARACTER

TRACE THEN COLOR
THE CUTE CHARACTER

TRACE THEN COLOR
THE CUTE CHARACTER

TRACE THEN COLOR
THE CUTE CHARACTER

TRACE THEN COLOR
THE CUTE CHARACTER

TRACE THEN COLOR
THE CUTE CHARACTER

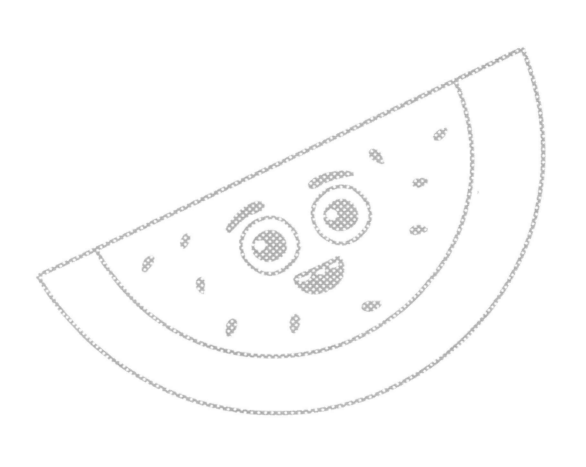

TRACE THEN COLOR
THE CUTE CHARACTER

TRACE THEN COLOR
THE CUTE CHARACTER

TRACE THEN COLOR
THE CUTE CHARACTER

TRACE THEN COLOR
THE CUTE CHARACTER

TRACE THEN COLOR
THE CUTE CHARACTER

TRACE THEN COLOR
THE CUTE CHARACTER

TRACE THEN COLOR
THE CUTE CHARACTER

Learn to draw the characters in this book in
How to Draw: Mermaids, Unicorns, and Other Cute Stuff
by Kevin Coulston

Available now on Amazon

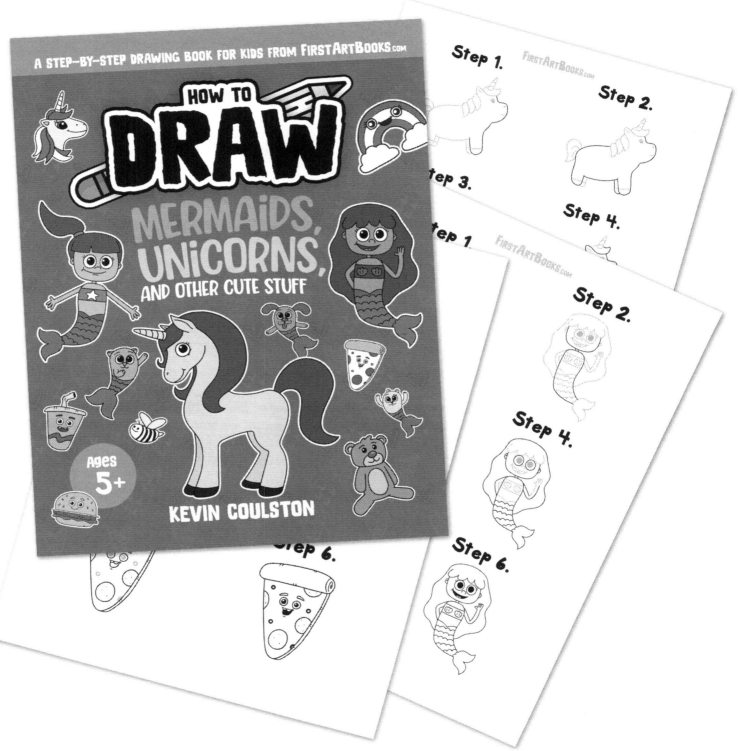

FirstArtBooks.com

Made in United States
Troutdale, OR
12/01/2024

25600687R00060